BROWNIE GROUNDHOG
and the FEBRUARY FOX

By
Susan Blackaby

Illustrated by
Carmen Segovia

🌳
STERLING
New York / London

On the second day of February, a groundhog named Brownie woke up.

She shimmied up the passageway of her cozy den and shoved aside the fluff of snow blocking her door. The air smelled sweet and cold.

When she stood up, her shadow stretched across the frosted field.

"I was afraid of that," said Brownie. "Shadows mean more winter, and more winter means waiting. Wait, wait, wait." Brownie stomped her foot. "Phooey!"

A small, scrawny fox heard Brownie grousing.
His ears twitched. He licked his chops and
crouched to pounce.

Before Brownie could take two steps, the fox knocked her flat. Brownie's basket went flying as they tumbled into a snow bank.

The fox panted and puffed.

"Hold still," he said. "I'm trying to eat you for breakfast."

"Don't be silly," said Brownie, wiggling free.

"You're too late for breakfast."

"Really?" The fox frowned. "What about lunch?"

"Too early," said Brownie. "You'll just have to wait."

"I hate waiting," said the fox.

"I know what you mean," said Brownie.

Brownie picked up her basket and crunched across the clearing, leaving tracks in the snow. The fox scampered along beside her.

"I don't suppose you've noticed any signs of spring," said Brownie.

The fox's tummy grumbled. "You," he said.

"Besides me," said Brownie.

"Then, no," said the fox.

Brownie listened for tweets and twitters but didn't hear any. She looked for shoots and sprigs but didn't see any.

"**Fiddle**," said Brownie.

"Not a single smidge of spring."

When they came to the pond, Brownie stopped to listen.

"Not a clink or a crackle," she said. "This icy ice is frozen solid."

Brownie sat down under a tree and scowled.

"Drat," she grumped. "Six weeks to wait and nothing to do."

"Lunch?" suggested the fox.

His little claws looked sharp. Brownie scooted out of reach.

"You can't eat yet," she said. "You haven't worked up an appetite."

"I *feel* appetitey," said the fox.

"Well, you aren't," said Brownie. "Why don't you clear the snow off the pond? That might do the trick."

The fox stepped onto the pond. He swept his
tail back and forth, sending up a snowy spray,
until the ice gleamed like green glass.

"Magnificent!" Brownie clapped. "Look what
you've done!"

"I've worked up an appetite," said the fox. He smiled, showing his pointy teeth.

"You've made a place to skate," said Brownie. She wrapped her scarf around her neck. "Come on," she said.

"Nothing works up an appetite like skating."

The fox grabbed Brownie by the tail as she slid onto the pond. They glided across the ice. They twirled and swirled. They looped and swooped. They skated figure eights until their knees buckled.

Gasping and giggling, they helped each other struggle up the bank.

"That was so much fun!" said Brownie.

"It was," said the fox, "and my appetite is all worked up."

Brownie bristled.

"No wonder," she said. "You skated right past lunch. Now you'll have to wait until dinner."

"*No*," moaned the fox. He hung his head. Even his tail sagged. "I want to eat you *now*. No more waiting."

"I know just how you feel," said Brownie.

Brownie steered the limp little fox over to a tree. She helped him sit down and tucked his fluffy tail around his feet. Then she wound her scarf around and around the fox's skinny middle, tying him to the trunk.

The fox tried to raise his paws. The scarf pulled tight.

"Stuck," he said, wriggling his shoulders.

Brownie grabbed her basket.

"**Good-bye!**" she said.

The fox stared **up** at her.

"You're leaving me?"

The fox threw his head back and howled.

Hoop, hoop, hoop
Piff, piff, piff

Brownie took three steps quickly up the path, glad to be on her way.

"Hoop, hoop, hoop," sobbed the fox.

Brownie took three more steps quite slowly, feeling a bit bad.

"Piff, piff, piff," whimpered the fox.

Brownie stopped and turned around.

"Oh, for Pete's sake," she said. "Stop crying. If you promise to keep your teeth to yourself, I'll make us a snack."

The fox sniffled. "I promise," he said. "What are we having?"

Brownie sat down and pulled a thermos out of her basket.

"Cocoa," she said. "Perfect for dunking cinnamon toast."

"Will I like it?" asked the fox.

"You'll love it," said Brownie. "Open up. And remember: No snapping."

Brownie dropped a tasty tip of soaky toast into the fox's mouth and then took one for herself.

While they traded bites, slurping and gulping, a robin stopped to peck at their crumbs scattered in the snow. She teased a piece of yarn from Brownie's scarf and then fluttered up into the tree.

"Look!" said Brownie.

"Our first sign of spring!"

"Besides you," said the fox.

When it was time to go, Brownie helped the fox to his feet.

"What are we doing tomorrow?" he asked.

"More waiting," said Brownie.

"Waiting and skating," said the fox. "Will you bring something yummy?"

"Something yummy to share," said Brownie.

And they headed for home.

For 'Greta, my first friend, and for Greg, obviously.
—S.B.

To Joan Manel
—C.S.

STERLING and the distinctive Sterling logo are registered trademarks of
Sterling Publishing Co., Inc.

Library of Congress Cataloging-in-Publication Data

Blackaby, Susan
Brownie Groundhog and the February Fox / by Susan Blackaby ; illustrated by Carmen Segovia.
p. cm.
Summary: Brownie the groundhog encounters a fox while waiting for winter to be over, and through clever maneuvering--
and tasty snacks--the two become friends.
ISBN 978-1-4027-4336-8
[1. Woodchuck--Fiction. 2. Foxes--Fiction. 3. Winter--Fiction.] I. Segovia, Carmen, ill. II. Title.
PZ7.B5318Br 2010
[E]--dc22

2009021559

Lot # :
2   4   6   8   10   9   8   7   5   3   1
03/10
Published by Sterling Publishing Co., Inc.
387 Park Avenue South, New York, NY 10016
Text © 2011 by Susan Blackaby
Illustrations © 2011 by Carmen Segovia
The artwork for this book was created using acrylic paint and ink.
The story is based on a character originally created by Carmen Segovia.
Distributed in Canada by Sterling Publishing
c/o Canadian Manda Group, 165 Dufferin Street
Toronto, Ontario, Canada M6K 3H6
Distributed in the United Kingdom by GMC Distribution Services
Castle Place, 166 High Street, Lewes, East Sussex, England BN7 1XU
Distributed in Australia by Capricorn Link (Australia) Pty. Ltd.
P.O. Box 704, Windsor, NSW 2756, Australia

Printed in China

Sterling ISBN 978-1-4027-4336-8

For information about custom editions, special sales, premium and
corporate purchases, please contact Sterling Special Sales
Department at 800-805-5489 or specialsales@sterlingpublishing.com.

Designed by Mina Chung